THE GOOD DOG

A Novella

Laura Stamps

The Good Dog

ISBN: 979-8-9875200-2-4 Paperback

Library of Congress Control Number: 2023902463

Permissions have been granted and filed by the publisher.
Publisher: Prolific Pulse Press LLC
Prolificpulse.com

Author Contact: laurastampsfiction.blogspot.com

Published March 2023 in Raleigh, North Caroline USA

Acknowledgements

Grateful acknowledgement is made to *Syncopation Literary Journal* and *Synchronized Chaos* in which parts of this novella first appeared.

The short story "To Be Loved" (Chapters 1-7 of this novella) was a Quarterfinalist in the *Able Muse Write Prize for Fiction 2022.*

Thank you to the reviewers who took the time to read *The Good Dog* and offer their kind words.

The Good Dog

1.

Don't know how it happened. Have no idea. But I'm obsessed with dogs. It's a new thing for me. This obsession. Relatively new. Just in the last month. Okay, maybe two months. Possibly three. Okay, four. Whatever. And not all dogs. Just small dogs. The smallest. Chihuahuas. I'm obsessed with Chihuahuas. And I have no idea why. Makes no sense. Absolutely none. The last thing I need is a dog. Dogs are too needy. Everyone knows that. Needy. Not what I want. Not what I need. Even from a dog. And yet, and yet. I seem to be obsessed. With these little Chihuahuas.

2.

But here's the thing. I know nothing about dogs. Don't even like dogs. Never wanted a dog. Never owned a dog. Well, not technically. Not me personally. Okay, we had a dog when I was in high school. A big dog. But it wasn't my dog. It was my brother's dog. Dogs were his thing. He was the one who wanted a dog. Not me. He was the one who promised to take care of it. Pleaded, begged, pestered our parents for a dog. Relentless, he was. Then one night dad took too many pills (he called them his "mood elevators"), ended up in the pet department at Richway (we still don't know how that happened), and bought a puppy. Pill poppers, my parents. Both of them. Mom was just as bad. Worse, even. Filled her prescription every month at the local pharmacy. One hundred pills at a time (what was her doctor thinking?). Those green and black capsules. Everywhere. All over the house. I'll never forget them. High anxiety. That's what she said she had. Too bad those pills never worked. On the anxiety. As for the high? Oh, yeah. Worked like a charm.

3.

We only had a dog for a year. Ran away the first chance it got. The quest for greener pastures, I suppose. Or maybe it just wanted to be fed. Dogs need to eat. And drink. It's important. But my brother wasn't so good at that. Or brushing or walking or playing with a dog. He was lousy at that too. It was probably the weed. Quite the doper, my brother. A year later we were dogless again. And my brother never mentioned dogs again. And dad. He never went to Richway again. But then he never remembered how he got there the first time. He was good at that. Never remembering. But that was dad.

4.

My best friend thinks my obsession with Chihuahuas is a guilt thing. Like I feel bad about the way my family treated that dog. Like I could make up for it by adopting a dog and taking good care of it. Like this would fix all the bad things that happened back then. To the dog. To me. To my brother. Like that would make everything right. But would it really? No. Not even close.

5.

And if you think I like being obsessed with Chihuahuas, think again. Just because I joined a national group for Chihuahua rescue on Facebook. Just because I comment with little hearts on all the posts for homeless and abused Chihuahuas. Just because I cruise my local Petco every week to look at dog sweaters. Just because I know the color, size, weight, age, and sex of the Chihuahua I would want if I wanted one (which I don't). If I ever adopted one (which I won't). None of that means anything. Nothing. Not a thing. Nada. Do you hear me?

6.

However, speaking of that Facebook group, you should have seen yesterday's post. The one about the tiny Chihuahua, the tan one (the color I want), four pounds (the weight I want), about three years old (the age I want), female (the sex I want) in a precious pink sweater. Such a tiny little thing. Tiny, tiny. And then there's this. This! She only has one eye. Can you imagine? Poor abused, neglected dog. Poor little Polly. That's her name. Fully vetted. Available for adoption. And she's in Dallas. Thirty minutes from where I live. How amazing is that? I hope a good person adopts her. She deserves it. A good person with a loving home. Someone who knows what it's like to be abused. To escape. To finally get away from the people who hurt you. Someone like me. But not me. Someone to spoil her. To give her more love than she can imagine. That. That's what Polly deserves.

Someone who likes dogs. Someone who wants a dog. A dog person. But not me. No. Not me.

7.

And yet, and yet. She's so adorable. In that little pink sweater. I do love those tiny dog sweaters. Too cute. Too bad I'm not interested. And I'm not. Well, maybe. One day. I don't know. Dallas is only thirty minutes away. Maybe I could go. Just to look. Nothing more. A good, loving person. Like me. But not me. A dog person. That's what Polly needs. Someone to love her. Like she deserves to be loved. Someone she can love. Like me. But not me. What do you think? Should I go? Maybe. I don't know. Okay. Just to look.

8.

Saturday morning. And I'm driving to PetSmart. In Dallas. Yes. I'm doing it. I'm actually doing this. I am. I'm pulling into the parking lot. Now. At PetSmart. I'm here. In Dallas. Can you believe it? Yes, I'm here. But just to look. A looker. That's what I am today. Nothing more. Just looking. That's all. I mean, really. What can it hurt, right?

9.

Barking. Loud barking. That's what I hear the minute I enter the store. It's all I hear. And this. This I'd like to know. How can anyone function in this? So much noise. So many dogs. Barking in their crates. Lots of them. Most of them. Barking. Loudly. Really loud. And people everywhere. Swarming like fire ants. Some in line at cash registers. Some with carts. People in every aisle. Shopping, shopping, shopping. But I'm not here for that. No. It's the dogs. Saturday is Adoption Day at PetSmart. The rescue group fostering Polly is here. Today. And I'm here too. Now. For Polly. But just to look. I'm a looker. Today. That's all. Nothing more.

10.

I make my way through the crowd. All these people. So many. It's crazy. I reach the back of the store. Finally. That's where the dogs are. But Polly. Where is she? I don't see her. Rows and rows of dogs. That's what I see.

Barking. Most of them. So many dog crates. One on top of the other. So many dogs. Fifty of them. At least. Maybe more. And loud. So loud.

11.

I join the line of people walking past the crates. Lookers. Just like me. Out on a Saturday. Looking at the dogs. And there are so many. So many dogs. And loud. Too loud. It's too much. Where is Polly? She's supposed to be here. That's what her Facebook post said. But I don't see her. This is impossible. Too many dogs. Too many people. Too much noise. It's overwhelming. To me. Triggering my anxiety. It is. I can feel it. Already. Oh, no. Pressure in my chest. Crushing pressure. Oh no, oh no. Polly. Where is she? Where?

12.

A woman walks toward me. A tag pinned to her shirt. She's one of the rescue people. "Excuse me," I say. "I'm looking for Polly. The Chihuahua on Facebook. The little dog with one eye." She smiles. A kind smile. Like she has x-ray vision. Like she can see all the way into my soul. Dear God, I hope not. How embarrassing. Anxiety is so inconvenient. "Yes," she says. "Miss Polly. Such a sweet little girl. But she's not here. We had over 200 applications for her from our Facebook post. Rather overwhelming, but very gratifying. She was adopted by one of those applicants." I smile and offer my congratulations. Do I look as disappointed as I feel? I hope not. How embarrassing. To come all this way. To Dallas. On a Saturday. For nothing. "Don't worry," the woman says, as if she really can see into my soul. "We've got another Chihuahua. And he's a sweetheart. You'll love him. Is that what you're looking for, a Chihuahua? If so, he's very special. Such a good dog."

13.

Looking? Yes, yes. A looker. Today. That would be me. "Yes," I say. "I'm just looking." That's all she needs to hear. The woman grabs my hand and tugs me toward the last crate. "Meet Walter," she says. I bend down to look in his crate. Yes, he's a Chihuahua. But he's black and brown (not the color I want). At least six pounds, maybe seven (not the weight I want). Too heavy. And he's a boy (not the sex I want). No, no, no. I'm not interested in male dogs. No. Not at all. If I were to adopt a dog (which I'm not), it would be a girl. Girls wear dresses. Cute little doggie dresses. Oh, how I love those dresses. Just looking at them makes me happy. Like the ones at my local Petco. All of them. Cute. So cute. My dog would wear dresses. Lots of them. Cute ones. Dresses are a must. Period.

14.

"Walter is the sweetest dog," the woman says. "Potty trained. Fully vetted. Low maintenance. Very friendly. Well behaved. Not a barker." How did she know? About the barking. That it bothers me. How? I stick my fingers through the bars of the crate. Walter sniffs my manicured hand (yes, I have a fabulous manicurist). He licks my fingers and wags his tail. Okay. She's right. He is friendly. I'll give her that. "I don't understand," I say. "If he's such a great dog, why hasn't he been adopted?" The woman shrugs. "Who knows?" she says. "It's probably his age. He's eight years old. Most people want a puppy. Not many adopt a dog like Walter. He's at that in-between stage. Too old to be a youngster. But not old enough to be a senior. We've had him for over a year. No interest in him whatsoever. It's a shame." Well, now I know. Walter is eight years old (not the age I want). He's too old. If I wanted to adopt a dog (which I don't), it wouldn't be a puppy. I'm not into puppy training. No. Not happening. But I wouldn't want an eight-year-old either. Okay. It's time to leave. Polly is gone. There's nothing for me here. I need to go home. Now. "Did you post about him on Facebook?" I say, trying to make a graceful exit. The woman opens the crate and lifts Walter out. He tinier than I thought. Definitely six pounds. But he looks as light as a wad of tissues. Walter snuggles into her arms and presses his head against her neck. "We did," the woman says. "No likes. No comments. No applications. Nothing."

15.

Oh, geez. How sad. Poor Walter. Now I really need to leave. To give these dog people a chance to hear about Walter. To adopt him. To give him a good home. Poor little boy.

16.

"Why don't you hold him?" the woman says, depositing Walter into my arms before I can stop her.

17.

Oh no, oh no, oh no. There's a dog in my arms. A dog! I can't believe she did that. What was she thinking? I'm just a looker. How could she forget? A looker. That's what I am. Nothing more. Oh, geez.

18.

Walter presses his paws against my chest and burrows into my arms. Sweetly. Calmly. Gently. No struggling. No panicking. No scratching. No squirming. It's as if he's completely unaware of my history with dogs. Like it doesn't matter to him that I've never held a little dog before. That my only dog was big. A big dog. And it wasn't even my dog. It was my brother's dog. Back in high school. Just for a year. One year. That's all. Fifteen years ago. I hold Walter tighter. How do you hold a Chihuahua? Can I hold him like a cat? I don't know! But this I do know. I can't drop him. Poor dog. Poor Walter.

The dog with the Facebook post no one liked. I can't add
to his misery. I can't. I can't drop him. Not in front of
this nice woman. Or all these dog people. In PetSmart.
How embarrassing!

19.

But what am I going to do? I can't leave. Not now. Not
with a dog in my arms (don't panic, don't panic, don't
panic). Anxiety is bad enough. But a panic attack? I
haven't had one of those in over a month. Maybe two
months. I forget. But I can't have one now. I can't. I
can't. Dear God, not now. Not in PetSmart. Please,
please, please! I need to think. What would my therapist
say? What? FOCUS. She'd tell me to focus. Focus on
something else. Like Walter. Yes. Focus, focus, focus.
On Walter. Okay. What about Walter? Well, he's light.
Surprisingly light. Like a box of tissue. Isn't that odd? I
think so. Six pounds. You'd think it would feel heavier.
But it doesn't. A six pound Chihuahua. Not that heavy at
all. Go figure.

20.

"Walter is such a special dog," the woman says, petting his tiny head. "So sad about him." Walter burrows deeper into my arms. "Sad?" I say. I don't understand. What could be worse than no one liking your Facebook post? Nothing. That's what. Absolutely. Nothing. But Walter's sad past is not my problem. Not now. I've got other concerns. Like how to get out of here. I mean, what can I do? What? I can't toss Walter into his crate, grab my purse, and run out of PetSmart. Okay, I could. But that would be stupid. A stupid thing for a thirty-year-old woman to do. Even though I want to. I really do. Really, really. I do.

21.

The rescue lady pulls a treat from her pocket and gives it to Walter. He gobbles it up. "Walter was surrendered by his owner," the woman says. "She adopted him when he was a puppy. But last year she was offered a better job in Georgia. She accepted the position and found an apartment in Atlanta. Unfortunately, pets were not allowed, so Walter had to go. She dropped him off at a city shelter in Fort Worth on her way out of town. And that's all I know. Poor Walter! To be abandoned at his age in a strange place with strange smells and strange dogs and strange people. He was confused and terrified when we found him. He couldn't stop shaking."

22.

Oh, geez. I had to ask.

23.

But everything turned out well in the end, didn't it? I mean, now he's with this nice woman. At PetSmart. Surrounded by dog lovers. Dog people. People who like dogs. People who want a dog. Not someone like me. I'm just looking. A looker. Nothing more. "But so many people are here today," I say. "Surely you've had some interest in him, yes?"

24.

"No," the woman says, giving Walter another treat from her pocket. "None. As usual."

25.

Then she smiles. A kind smile. Like she can see right through me. All the way to my soul. Dear God!

26.

"A dog is better than a husband," the woman says. "Did you know that?" Wait a minute. Wait. A. Minute. Where did that come from? Where? "Excuse me?" I say. Maybe I misunderstood. Surely I did. The woman looks down at Walter and laughs. He's snoring. In my arms. Fast asleep. What? When did that happen? "It's true," she says. "Dogs are more consistent with their affection. They're not moody. Or manipulative. Or perfectionists. Or worriers. Or egomaniacs. Or judgmental. Dogs will never abandon you. They just love you. All the time. That's what they do. And they're excellent listeners." She winks at me. "How many men can you say that about?"

27.

Oh, geez. The story of my life. How did she know? Moody, self-absorbed men. Too many of them. In my past. Like my ex-husband, Earl. The hypochondriac. Divorced him six months ago. Best decision I've made in years. Good riddance, I say. Never had anxiety until I married Earl. Or panic attacks. Didn't even know what they were. But I do now. Thanks to seven years of marriage. Should have divorced Earl years ago. Why didn't I? Why, why, why? My girlfriends say it's my heart. It's too big. Too soft. They think it's a curse. In Earl's case, it was. But no more. I'm done with men like that. All of them. Selfish, manipulative worriers. Done. With. Them.

28.

"Did you see this?" the woman says, pointing to the information sheet attached to Walter's crate. "All our older dogs like Walter are half price today. And he's such a good dog. No trouble at all."

29.

An hour later the Dallas skyline fades from my rearview mirror on the drive home to Irving. I did it. I escaped. Finally. But my checking account is three hundred dollars lighter. And there's a big shopping bag from PetSmart in my backseat. And a new pet carrier in the trunk. And there's Walter. In the passenger seat. Wrapped in a blanket. Cozy in his new dog bed. Chewing on a dental bone. Happily. Peacefully. As if we've been together for years.

30.

"Tell me this," I say to Walter. "Is a dog really better than a husband?" I turn off the highway onto the exit ramp leading up to Irving. Walter drops the bone and climbs into my lap. Gently. Calmly. Like he's been doing it for years. He rests his head on my arm and looks up at me. "Should I take that as a Yes?" I say. "Okay then. Good to know."

31.

Three weeks. Only three. That's all it took. Just three weeks to discover everything the rescue lady said about dogs was true. And Walter. More than true. Mcre. Everything. All of it. True.

32.

"I should get you one of these," I say to Walter. "What do you think?" I'm on the couch, flipping through the latest issue of my favorite dog magazine. Yes, I subscribe to dog magazines now. Yes, I have a favorite. I know, I know. What's happening to me, right? What? It's crazy. I'm totally out of control. This dog addiction of mine. Out of control. Completely. In just three weeks. And I'm happy. For the first time in a long time. So happy. I point to the article about car seats for dogs. Just. Too. Cute. "Do you want one?" I say. Walter is rolling around on the couch next to me, wrestling with his toy monkey. He stops, looks up at the magazine I'm waving over his head, and tosses the monkey into my lap. "I'll take that as a Yes," I say. I know, I know. I even speak "dog" now. It's crazy. The effect this dog has had on me. Truly. Amazing. "We'll get you a doggie car seat," I say. "Soon. But not today. We need to go. Can't be late for your first appointment with the groomer."

33.

But, but, but, now it's ringing. My cell phone. I glance at the number. Oh, geez. Not again. Should I answer it? Yes. Time to put a stop to this. Once and for all. I hope, I hope. "What?" I say to the last person on earth I want to talk to. Ever. In this lifetime. The. Last. Person. "Happy Saturday to you too," Earl says. "Cranky much?" I ignore him and look at my watch. Five minutes. That's all I can give him. Then I'm hanging up. "Earl, this has to stop," I say. "You've called me four times this week. Five times last week. And every day the week before. We're divorced, remember? Deal with it. Get a life, Earl. I did. Goodbye." Three minutes. Then I'm hanging up. "Ashley, wait," Earl says. "Don't go. This is important." I look at my watch. Two minutes. That's it. I can't be late. Not today. Not for this groomer. Walter needs a bath, nail trim, dental, the works. This groomer is supposed to be the best in town. She came highly recommended. And I guess she is. The best. It took three weeks to get in to see her. And today is the day. No way I'm letting Earl blow this for me. Not happening. Not today.

34.

"I hear you have a dog," Earl says. What? What did he just say? How does he know? "Who told you that?" I say. Walter climbs into my lap and rests his head on my chest. Poor little guy. I bet he can hear my heart. Pounding. I know he can. Anxiety. It's always like this with Earl. "No one," Earl says. "I saw you coming out of your apartment a few days ago, and you were walking a dog. Ashley, I can't believe you did this. A dog? Of all the crazy stunts! What were you thinking? And how long were you planning to keep this a secret from me?" Oh, great. He's stalking me again. Bummer. On the other hand, Earl hates dogs. I can only imagine. His face. That look. When he saw Walter. When he realized I have a dog. The horror of it. That had to be worth a million dollars. I laugh out loud. I shouldn't. But I do. Can't help it. Sorry. Not really. I scoop Walter up and glance at my watch. Earl just ran out of time. "Two things," I say. "First, stop stalking me. Second, my dog is none of your business. We're divorced, Earl. I have a new life. You're not in it. Goodbye."

35.

"Ashley," Earl says. "Don't hang up! That's not why I called. This is an emergency. There's something wrong with my arm." I slip Walter into his harness, attach his leash, and grab my purse. "So?" I say. Nothing like having a hypochondriac for an ex-husband. Everything is an emergency. So predictable. Him. "I found a bump on my arm," Earl says. "It's red and itchy. Really itchy. It looks like a pea, but it's hard as a rock. I researched it on WebMD. I have all the symptoms of a cancerous tumor. Ashley, I don't know what to do. It's Saturday, and my doctor's office is closed on the weekends. I can't get in to see him until Monday. I need you to take a look at it and tell me what you think." I find my keys, wrap Walter's leash around my wrist, and head toward the door. "Earl, what do I always tell you?" I say. "Stay away from the WebMD site. It just makes you crazy. As for your bump, it sounds like a mosquito bite. Maybe hives. That's all. You're not dying. You don't have cancer. And I'm not looking at it. We're not married, Earl. Not anymore. Go to the Minute Clinic at CVS. Let the nurse tell you it's a mosquito bite. I'm hanging up now. Gotta go. Goodbye, Earl." I open the door, stop, and turn around. One last look at the apartment. Do I have everything I need for the groomer? I hope so.

36.

"But what if you're wrong," Earl says. "What if it's cancer? You'll be sorry. You know you will. Ashley, I could die! I was up all night worrying about this. Cancer kills. Everyone knows that. And if I die from this, it'll be your fault. And you'll have to live with that for the rest of your life. Do you really want my death hanging over your head?" Earl says. He sighs into the phone. Loudly. Dramatically. Like he's dying. Like I just murdered him. "Everything isn't always all about you," Earl says. "What a cold, uncaring person you are! You've always been that way. I ask you for help, and what do you do? You ignore my symptoms. Early detection saves lives. You know it does. How could you be so cruel to me?"

37.

Oh, geez. Here we go again. Nothing ever changes. The cup is always half empty with him. Depressing, stressful, such a downer. That's Earl. I guide Walter into the hallway and close the door. "I'm leaving now," I say. "Goodbye, Earl. Don't call me again. Ever." I lock the door, and Walter trots toward the stairs. He knows the drill. Such a good dog. "I can't believe I married you," Earl says. "A vicious, manipulative, selfish woman. That's what you are. You only care about yourself. It's no wonder I divorced you!" I stop and stare at my cell phone. The man is certifiable. "Goodbye, Earl," I say. "Don't call me again. Ever. And get your facts straight. I divorced YOU!"

38.

I hang up. Walter is sitting at my feet. Patiently. Calmly. He's such a good dog. "That went well, didn't it?" I say. "Looks like Earl is stalking me. Us. Again. This crazy person. My ex. Oh, geez. Welcome to my life, Walter. Aren't you glad I adopted you?"

39.

Three hours later I'm twirling. Love it. Always have. Since elementary school. Twirling, twirling. And I still do. Like right now. Twirling across the living room floor. A freshly groomed pup in my arms. His fur sweetly scented with strawberry shampoo. Who knew dancing with a Chihuahua could be so much fun? And singing. I sing while I twirl. Always. "Still alive and well," I sing, twirling with Walter. In my living room. Dancing to Johnny Winter. My favorite album from the 70s. I sing to Walter. Such a sweet boy. I sing because all went well with the new groomer this morning. I sing because it's Saturday. Because I have the weekend off from my job at the hotel. Because nothing beats Johnny Winter on vocals and Rick Derringer on guitar. The best of the best on electric guitar. That they were. Hands down. The. Best.

40.

So handsome. My Walter. When I picked him up from the groomer. She'd tied a little bandana around his neck. Her finishing touch. Lovely. Really. But the only bandana small enough to fit Walter today was a flowery Christmas pattern. Bright red poinsettias. The groomer hoped I didn't mind. After all, Walter is a boy. And it's only June. "No worries," I said. "I love poinsettias." And I do. Really. But what I didn't say is how much I despise Christmas. Dread it. Truly. No fan of the holidays. No. Not me. Or winter. Too cold. Give me Texas heat any day. Give me humidity. Give me sunshine. Summer. Give me summer. Days so hot I can jump in the car with wet hair. Drive to work. Arrive dry. Brush and go. That's the life. The. Life. Try that in the winter. You'll get popsicle head. You will. Ask me. I know.

41.

No fan of holiday shoppers. No. Not me. Crazy people. That they are. Like last December. In Target. The power flickered the minute I entered the store. "I don't care if the lights go out completely," the woman behind me said. "I'm getting my Christmas shopping done no matter what!" Where do these people come from? Where? Just breathe, lady. Just. Breathe.

42.

No fan of Christmas decorations. No. Not me. Although it wasn't always that way. Before Earl. Before seven years of marriage. I loved the holidays. Wrapping presents. Decorating the tree. But then Earl. The first year. He hated my Christmas tree. The second year. He complained we had no holiday decorations. Outside. The third year. He yelled at me for spending a few dollars to decorate. Outside. I gave up after that. No point to it. Nothing was ever good enough. For Earl. Nothing. Ever. No. Not a thing.

43.

But, but, but. Now I have Walter. This year. This Christmas. This first year after the divorce. "We should celebrate," I say to Walter. "Get a tree. Decorate. We should. What do you think?" Walter reaches up and licks my neck. Such a sweet boy. My twirling partner. The best. He is. "I'll take that as a Yes," I say. Yes, we should dance for the holidays this year. And sing. Sing to my favorite Christmas album. To Lauren Daigle's New Orleans jazz. Yes. And twirl. Yes, yes. Lots of that. Like today. With my freshly groomed pup. Twirling across the living room floor. Twirling because I'm free.

Because I'm still alive and well. Because that's good enough. For me.

44.

"Pretty quiet last night," the night auditor says when I arrive. It's Monday morning. Early. The Longview Hotel. That's where I work. As a desk clerk. First shift. That's me. This isn't just a job. No. It's my career. And I'm proud of it. I worked lots of jobs to get through college. But desk clerking was the only one I enjoyed. Still do. So I stayed with it. Made a career out of it. Hey, how many people can say they like what they do for a living? Not many. Well, I can. And I do. "Quiet nights are good," I say, pushing my purse and lunch bag into the little cabinet beneath the front desk. There's a trick to happiness in this profession. Know your strengths and weaknesses. Like uniforms. I despise them. More. More than that. Hate. Much better word. Why? Pantyhose. Uniforms for women almost always mean pantyhose. Forget it. Not wearing them. No. Not me. Torture devices. That's what they are. Trust me. I know. I've worked at some of the big chain hotels. The ones that require uniforms. Ramada, Howard Johnson, Marriott, you name it. But no more. I made a vow to myself. No more uniforms. Or pantyhose. Now I only work at hotels where I can dress in street clothes. Jeans, a nice shirt, comfortable shoes. That's it. That's me. Yes, those hotels tend to be smaller. Yes, they pay less. But worth every penny in comfort. Trust me. This. This I know.

45.

"Before I forget," the night auditor says, "I need to tell you something."

46.

Hours are another thing. Two years ago my boss offered me the night auditor position. I turned it down. More pay. True. But the hours stink. Forget third shift. Vampire hours. No thanks. Give me sunshine. Give me daylight. I'm a first shift girl. Like I said. Know your strengths and weaknesses. And flow with them.

47.

"I saw Earl," the night auditor says, slipping off her sweater before walking out the door. It's June. Sizzling hot outside. Already. But the air conditioner at the front desk only has one setting: Freezing. "Where?" I say. Actually, who cares? Not me. The less I hear about Earl the better. "In the parking lot," the auditor says, pointing to the space next to the big azalea bush. "Right there. He had a clear view of the office. He was watching you. I'm sure of it. I walked by his car just to make sure. And he was watching you alright. It was last Wednesday. The day I came by to pick up my paycheck, remember?" I do. Remember. The boss always leaves the night auditor's check with me. I handed it to her that day. Yes. I remember. "Earl is stalking me again," I say, rolling my eyes. "He called on Saturday. Told me all about it. Let me know he's been watching me. At my apartment. And now. Here too. I guess. How aggravating! The man is such a pest. But harmless. I think. I hope. But a pest all the same. Anyway, thanks for telling me. Good to know."

48.

According to my therapist, Earl triggers me. The anxiety. The panic attacks. He's the cause of it. All of it. In fact, he's the reason I'm seeing a therapist. Never needed one before. Never considered it. Before Earl. Before the divorce. Before the anxiety appeared. And the panic. Those awful attacks. My therapist says I couldn't process how bad it was with Earl while we were still married. I was in survival mode. That's all I could do. Survive. But after. After the divorce. Then. That's when it hit me. All of it. Like a flood. Overwhelmed me. Emotionally. Mentally. And Earl just makes it worse. Now. The way he triggers me. The way he enjoys doing it. A narcissist. That's what he is. According to my therapist, narcissists love to torment people. Especially the brave ones. Those who leave them. Like me. Thing is. I've never considered myself a brave person. Never thought leaving him was brave. I just couldn't take it anymore. That's all. Just. Couldn't. Such a negative person. He is. So depressing. The things he said to me. Pulling me down. Every day. Every chance he got. He was killing my soul. That's how it felt. Painful. Too painful. So I left. To save myself. Save. Me. Had to. No choice.

49.

But that's the problem. Earl isn't gone. Not entirely. He's still in my life. Still reappearing. Pestering, pestering. Triggering me. He'd never harm me. Physically. I don't think. Hope not. But still. My therapist says I'll never heal from the anxiety and panic until Earl is out of my life. Gone. Completely. She calls it "going no contact." It's the last step in my healing process. A step I need to take. Want to. But can't. I mean, how do I do that? How do I get Earl out of my life? Completely out. How? When he continues to call me. Text. Stalk me. And yet I'm the one who's supposed to do this? No contact. Me? How? This. This is my question. This I'd like to know. How do I go no contact with Earl? How do I do that? How?

50.

"Earl needs someone to give him a lesson on the meaning of divorce," the night auditor says, laughing as she stuffs her sweater into her backpack. "I'm thinking a cop with a restraining order." She laughs even louder. "Can you imagine the look on Earl's face?"

51.

This. This is why I like her. This is why she's one of my best friends.

52.

Now I'm laughing too.

53.

"I'm not surprised," my therapist says at our Wednesday session. When I tell her about Earl's call. When I tell her what the night auditor said. That Earl is stalking me. Again. "Why isn't this working?" I say. "I thought if I answered his calls. Not all of them. Not every time. But most of the time. If I told him to stop calling me. That I have a new life. That he's not a part of it. That he'd get a clue and move on. Leave me alone. That he'd get tired of me. Rejecting him. Every time. That he'd give up. Eventually. But, no. I just made things worse, didn't I?

What am I going to do? What? I can't live like this. I can't. And I shouldn't have to. Really. I shouldn't. But what can I do?"

54.

This is all my fault. I know it is. When am I going to learn? When? When will I stop being so nice? To everyone. To bad-news people. To those who don't deserve it. Giving them a zillion chances to mess up. To run over me. To take advantage. Like Earl. Especially Earl. He's never going to change. Is he? No. He's not. Narcissists never change. That's what my therapist says. And Earl won't either. He'll never change. Never. But what can I do? What? This is terrible!

55.

"Relax, Ashley," my therapist says. "You still have options. You know you do. Let's talk about those options. Do you have any ideas? Think about it." I lean back in my chair. Thank God, she's not one of those therapists you see in the movies. You know the kind. The ones that make their clients lie down on a couch. No way I'd do that. Lie down. On a couch. Can't. Can't do that. Not with my therapist. It's her voice. Too calm. Too soothing. Too sensible. Knowing me, I'd get too comfortable. Fall asleep on her couch. Start snoring. Oh, geez. Can you imagine? How embarrassing!

56.

"First I need to tell you something," I say. "It was horrible. This nightmare. The one I had last night. Really scary. I dreamed I was in a house with a bunch of people. Can't remember how many. Five or six. Something like that. A small dinner party. In a big house. Suddenly, there was a crashing sound in another part of the house. And shouting. And gunfire. Robbers were breaking into the house. We knew they'd find us at any minute. Everyone at the dinner party was terrified. Me too. We were frozen with fear. All of us. But I knew we couldn't just sit there and wait for the robbers to find us and rob us. Or attack us. Or worse. We had to do something. We had to get out of there and go for help. I tried to get everyone to stop panicking and come with me. To escape. To make a run for it. But they couldn't.

Too scared. No one could move. Only me. So I jumped up and slipped out the back door. I ran as fast as I could through every yard in the neighborhood, looking for someone to help us. But no one was home. All the houses were empty. So I ran into the woods. By then the robbers were after me. Chasing me. All I could do was run. Run and run and run. It was terrifying. And that's what woke me up. My breathing. I could hear myself panting loudly in bed while I ran for my life. What a horrible nightmare. Just awful. Still gives me goosebumps. What do you think it means? Anything? Do you know? What?"

57.

My therapist smiles. "Ashley, you already know what it means," she says. What? What? Where did that come from? Why would I ask a question if I already know the answer? "Think about it," she says. "Start with the robbers. Who do you think they represent? Who do you know that wants to capture you? To hold your life hostage? To steal your time? To never give you a moment's peace? Who attacks you verbally every chance he gets? Who have you been running from for the last year? Who is after you now?"

58.

Oh, geez.

59.

I've changed my mind. A therapist's couch looks pretty good right now. Then I could roll over. Bury my face in the pillow. And moan.

60.

"Earl," I say. I moan anyway. Why not? I deserve it. A good moan. It feels great. I should do it again. But that would be rude. Or dramatic. Or both. Okay. I won't.

61.

"Exactly," my therapist says. "Earl."

62.

"I give up," I say. "I can't take this anymore. Let's do it. Tell me how to go no contact. It's time. I'm ready now. I think. I hope. Can I do this? Maybe. Can I? I have to. I do. Oh, geez, this is going to be hard."

63.

Before I leave, I stop by the receptionist's desk to schedule my next appointment. In my purse is the information my therapist gave me about all the ways to go no contact. Now it's up to me to choose one. Or two. Or all of them. My decision. Me. Good God, this is going to be hard!

64.

But wait. Wait. A. Minute. Something is wrong. "Your hair," I say to the receptionist. "You colored it. Again. Very nice." She thanks me. But there's no joy in her eyes. No light. What? What? She's the most cheerful person I know. A beacon of light. That's what she is. Full of joy. And energy. That's her. But not today. There's no light coming out of her. No sizzle. Not even a spark. "Something awful happened to you, didn't it?" I say. "Are you okay?" It's her hair. It's a stylish shade of brown streaked with blonde highlights. Very pretty.

Very normal. Except, except. She's anything but normal. No. Not her. She's the woman with hot pink hair. Or orange. Or blue. Or green. Or purple. Never brown. Never normal. Not her. No. Never. She lives for colorful hair. Drives all the way to Galveston every four months to have it done. Pays her colorist $300 to do it. Swears it's worth every penny. Totally. Worth it. To be a blaze of brilliant color. A beacon of light. Every time she enters a room. But not now. Not today. I was right. Something is very wrong.

65.

"I left my boyfriend," the receptionist says. "We were together for eight years. It was a bad breakup. Really bad. But I had to do it." Sadness. She's drenched in it. And now she looks like she could cry. Oh, geez. I could cry. This is awful. She needs a hug. And I'm a hugger. But am I allowed to do that? Can therapy patients hug the staff? What is the protocol for that? The rules? What, what? "When I left him I made a decision," she says. "To become a different person. A new me. I didn't want anything to remain of the old me. Nothing to remind me of the woman I used to be. The woman I was with him. The woman that wasted eight years of her life. As far as I'm concerned, that woman is dead and gone. Good riddance. That's what I say."

66.
Wow.

67.
Forget protocol. Forget the rules. She needs a hug. So I give her one. A big one. And she clings to me. Like I'm a life raft. Like she's drowning. I know the feeling. I hug her tighter. Just for that. "This is the new me," she says. "Everything has changed. My hair, my makeup, my clothes, all of it. I live in a new apartment in a different part of town. I have a new cell phone number, email address, and Facebook account. There's nothing left of the old me. That woman is history. Good riddance!" Got to hand it to her. Talk about guts. She's got them. I give her another hug. Just for that. "You're so courageous," I say. "And brave. A brave woman. That's what you are. Leaving him was a brave thing to do. Reinventing

yourself was a brave thing to do. Everything you did was brave. So brave. And courageous. You're amazing. Do you know that?"

68.

She smiles. And there it is. A spark of light. I see it. A tiny one. But it's there. "Thanks," she says. "Some men are just bad news. He was one of them. I always knew that. But he had so much potential. I just kept hoping he would change. That he'd grow up one day and become the good guy I knew he could be if he wanted to. But after eight years I realized he doesn't want to change. He likes being bad news. Knowing that, you'd think it would be easier to leave him, right? But it wasn't. It was hard. Really hard. And it hurt. It still hurts. I spent a large chunk of my life with him. All my dreams for the future were tied up with him. Leaving that behind hurt more than I thought it would." She shrugs. "But it was the right thing to do. And now I'm free. Now I can build a happy future for myself. Now I can do good things for me. I deserve that."

69.

"You're my hero," I say. "Truly."

70.

Tonight I'm making a salad for dinner. My favorite salad. Two cups of frozen broccoli, cauliflower, and carrots steamed in the microwave and chilled in the refrigerator. A head of chopped romaine lettuce. A bag of red butter lettuce. Vegan ranch dressing. A dash of garlic salt. Toss everything thoroughly in a big salad bowl. And what do you have? Lip-smacking perfection. Tasty. So tasty. I love being vegan. Can you tell? I do. Why? Because vegans love to eat. Me too. And vegans eat a lot. Me too. Yes. These are my people.

71.

"I've had an epiphany," I say to Walter while we eat. "Earl is bad news. He's one of those bad-news men." Walter looks up from his bowl of kibble. "I need to be free too," I say. "Free of him. Free to build a happy future for myself. Free to do good things for me. I deserve that. I do."

72.

No contact means no contact. I can no longer answer Earl's calls (even the desperate ones). No longer respond to his text messages (even if he says he's dying, which he isn't). No longer answer his emails (no matter what horrible deed he accuses me of this time). No face-to-face meetings (no matter how much he begs, pleads, or threatens). No contact of any kind. Nada. None. Zero. It's over.

73.

Good riddance!

74.

That's what I say.

75.

"This no contact thing isn't working," I say to Walter two weeks later. "I knew it would be hard. I knew Earl would freak. And he has. But he's still not getting the message. He's not. Even though I've blocked his calls, texts, and emails. But what can I do? What? This is crazy. He's crazy. Any suggestions?"

76.

"Here's a thought," I say to Walter when he climbs into my lap. He enjoys our discussions. I know he does. "If Earl can act like a crazy person, I can too," I say. "Wild and crazy. The new me. Why not? It's certainly not the old me. The exact opposite. That's what it is. But maybe I need a new me too. Like the receptionist at my therapist's. But, but, but. I don't know. Although it does sound like fun. Doesn't it? Wild and crazy. Could I pull it off? I don't know. I guess. I could. But what does it mean? For me. Wild and crazy. No clue. But it can't be that hard. Right? What do you think? Any suggestions?"

77.

Walter rolls over in my lap. I scratch the soft fur on the top of his head. He's such a good listener. Discussions with him are always productive. "It's not like I don't have something in common with her," I say. "I do. For example. She left her long-term relationship. And I left

mine. Eight years for her. Seven years for me. But then.
She took the next step. I didn't. That's the difference."

78.

And it's a big one. Big difference. She reinvented herself
and her life. All of it. And I didn't. I just moved. Out of
the house Earl and I owned. And into this apartment. I
had to. Had to get out of there. Had to get away from
him. Didn't take much with me either. Didn't want to.
Just my collection of jazz CDs. Favorite books. A few
dishes. Personal items. My clothes. Just enough to fill up
my car. That's it. All I wanted. To this furnished
apartment. It's all I need.

79.

But I had other issues to deal with too. Of course. Other
baggage. Heavy, heavy stuff. Like anxiety. And panic
attacks. Thanks to Earl. Useless junk. All of it. But there
it was. After Earl. After I left him.

80.

But, but, but. What if?

81.

"What if I took the next step now?" I say to Walter. "To a new me. A new life. Could I do that? A wild and crazy me. What do you think? Could I? Possibly. I'm finally in a good place. In life. My life. To do it. Now. I think. Maybe. But how? How do you take the next step? Wild and crazy. How did she do it? The receptionist. How?"

82.

Walter looks at me. I look at him. Not. A. Clue.

83.

"I guess you heard," the night auditor says when I arrive for my shift on Monday morning. Such a dreary day. Today. Cloudy. Chance of rain. Or so they say. No fan of it. Rain. No. Not me. Not with the temperature over a hundred degrees. Like it has been all week. Like it will be again today. Heat storms. Not good. Trust me. No fun. Pray for the power to stay on. That's what I do. It's all I ask. All day long.

84.

"Hear what?" I say. The night auditor hands me an official-looking flyer. "The owner sold the hotel," she says. "Hope you have some money put away. You'll need it. Looks like we're all out of a job at the end of the month." She points to the flyer in my hand. "Everyone gets one of these today," she says. "It's the press release for the sale. The new owner is bringing in his own staff. And you know how that goes. They're in. We're out." She opens the door of the lobby and looks outside. "What a crappy way to start the week," she says. "Oh, great. It's starting to rain. Perfect. I hate Mondays."

85.

Before I can reply, she dashes out the door and sprints across the parking lot to her car. Good luck with that. Now it's pouring. Sheets of rain. Lashing the windows of the lobby. Heat storms. God help us.

86.

Rain continues to pound the parking lot. I watch and think. I never saw this coming. The sale. Of the hotel.

But you never do. On the other hand, I'm not surprised. Not really. It happens all the time in this business. And it's not the first for me. Even a chain hotel will dump its entire staff when new management takes over. It happens. Not a big deal. Not this time. Not for me. I'm okay. Financially. For now. Money from the sale of the house (my divorce settlement) went into an IRA. And there's my savings account. I deposit a little each month. Not much. But it adds up. Because you never know. Because things happen. Like emergencies. Like job loss. Like today. Because, because. Life. It can get weird. It can. Seven years with Earl taught me that.

87.

But here's the thing. Now what? That's the question. What's next for me? What should I do? Who should I be? What? And this. The most important thing. How brave am I? Brave enough to reinvent myself? To create a new life. A new me. A wild and crazy me. Could I? Possibly. Maybe. Yes? Yes? I don't know. But I want to. I do.

88.

After work I stop by CVS. I'm out of shampoo. Oh, geez. They've rearranged the store. Again. Lovely. Why do they do that? Why? And where did they put the shampoo this time? It's not where it used to be. All I see are boxes and boxes of hair color. And no shampoo. And this. Tell me this. Why do all the models on hair color boxes look gorgeous? And why do they all have perfect hair? In the perfect color? Nobody has perfect hair. No one. Women know this. We all do. So why do they think they can fool us? I pick up one of the boxes. Wow. Okay. That's a beautiful shade of red. I put it back on the shelf. I have to confess. I've always wanted to be a redhead. Me. Secretly. Always. My secret. Mine. There's just something about red hair. You know? Not crimson red. Not ruby red. Not strawberry-pink (are you kidding me?). Just a nice shade of red. Like auburn. Or burgundy. Subtle. But pretty. Like the model on the cover of this box. Just like her. Wow. That's a gorgeous shade of red. Really. But how would it look? How? This color. On me. Wild and crazy. That's how. But, but, but. What if? I really love it. I do. What if? Okay. Why not? I grab the box, dash to the cash register, pay for it, and run outside. Into the rain. With no shampoo. Oh, geez. What have I done?

89.

"Is my hair too long?" I say to Walter. He's rolling around on the bathroom rug, gnawing on a bully stick. "It's too long. Isn't it? For this hair color. I think it is. Possibly. I mean, I've never done this before. Colored my hair. So I don't know. Is there enough dye in this box for my hair? For waist-length hair? Like mine. Oh, geez. What if there isn't? I could end up with weird hair. Red on top and brown on the bottom. Or streaked hair. Or worse. Ruined hair. Just what I need. Geez. This could be awful. Horrible. A disaster. What am I doing? I don't know!"

90.

Walter ignores me. No human can compete with a bully stick.

91.

"Okay," I say. "How about this? I could cut my hair. Possibly. Maybe. I'm considering it. Shoulder-length hair. How would that look on me? Maybe I could even cut bangs. Haven't had bangs since high school. What do you think?" Walter continues to ignore me. Now he's growling at his bully stick. Dog happiness. Totally. I love seeing him like this. He's such a sweetie. My dog. The best. I should buy that brand again for him. "Well, it's not like I don't know how to do it," I say. "I do. I cut my hair in high school. All the time. Bought a haircutting book from my mother's mail order book club. But that was fifteen years ago. Haven't cut my hair since. I'm thinking waist-length hair is just too long. For coloring. I'd need two boxes to do it. I bet. I would. But I only bought one. So now what? I have no choice. If I want to color my hair, I'll have to cut it first. And if I want to reinvent myself, I should go all the way. Cut bangs too. Right? Why not? Or should I? I don't know. This could be a mistake. Awful. Horrible. What do you think?"

92.

Walter tosses his bully stick at my feet, pounces on it, and rolls over on my foot to finish his treat. "You're right," I say. "I'll do it. Thanks for the advice. You're so good at that."

93.

Like I said. Life is weird. My job of three years will be terminated at the end of this month. And the lease I signed on my apartment will expire at the end of this month. What are the odds? Right? Old doors closing. New doors opening. That's what my therapist would say. But I say life is just plain weird.

94.

"I like the idea of a new you," my therapist says at our next session. "Even a wild and crazy you. But how do you plan to make that happen?" I lean back in my chair. Where is a therapist's couch when you need it? "Your guess is as good as mine," I say. "Totally clueless. That's me. Not that I haven't thought about it. I have. A lot. But let's face it. I have no experience being wild and crazy. Zero. None. I'm the good girl, remember? The one who always takes care of everyone else. The one who never turns a needy person down. Not even the bad-news people. Not even those I should walk away from. My heart goes out to all of them. Wild and crazy. What's that? A strange land. That's what it is. To me. Uncharted territory. Seriously. No idea how to get there. Not a clue. I need a map. Something. Anything. You're the therapist. You've got maps. Right? Can you give me one?"

95.

"I do," my therapist says. "I've got the map. But first you need to ask yourself this question. Wild and crazy is a radical change for you. Do you really want to go there? Or is this just a daydream? Think about it, Ashley. Is wild and crazy a change you really want to make?"

96.

Yes," I say. "I do. I think. There's something about it. You know? It appeals to me. For some strange reason. I

can't stop thinking about it. The possibilities call to me.
Yes. That's my answer. That's what I want. Wild and
crazy. Something totally different. A new me. A new
life. Completely new. Yes. That's what I want."

97.

This time I leave my therapist's office with an index
card. On it she's written one question. If I could live
anywhere, where would it be? That's the question. Too
bad I don't know the answer. Especially since she says
the answer to this question is the map to the land of wild
and crazy. What? What? What kind of sense does that
make? None. Zero. That's what. No sense at all. Sounds
like a bunch of mumbo jumbo therapist babble to me. I
mean, how could my answer to this question be a map?
It can't. Are you kidding me? Please. This is why I
rarely understand anything she says. And I pay her for
this. Geez!

98.

"Cool hair," the night auditor says when I arrive the next
morning for my shift. "If we weren't friends I'd be

jealous. Seriously. Who knew you had a natural wave in your hair? That's so not fair. Not when I'll need perms for the rest of my life. Not fair at all. In fact, I've changed my mind. I am jealous. So there." This. This is why we're friends. We're both losing our jobs next week. But she can still make me laugh. "You're nuts," I say. "Anyway, it was just an experiment." She tucks her sweater into her backpack. "Maybe so, but it worked," she says. "Lucky you. So what are you going to do next week? I'm already applying at other hotels. How about you?" I pull up a chair and sit down to review the list of reservations for today. Looks like a busy afternoon. "Not yet," I say. "My apartment lease expires next week too. Don't know what I'm going to do about that either." She slings her backpack over her shoulder and heads toward the door. "You're so lucky," she says. "You're finally free. Do you realize that? No job to tie you down. No lease to keep you here. You could do anything. Go anywhere. Opportunities like that don't come around too often." I look up from the list of reservations. "True," I say. "Either I'm finally free or life is just plain weird." She laughs. "Leave it to you," she says on her way out.

99.

"Travel," I say to my therapist at our next session. I show her the index card. Travel. That's what I've written on the card. "If I could live anywhere, where would it be?" I say. "That's the question you asked me. The answer is I still don't know. Here's the thing. I've never been out of Texas. How can I know where I'd like to live? I've never been anywhere. Never seen anything. Just Texas. So travel is my answer. I can't answer your question until I see more of the country. Maybe then I'll know what my answer will be. Maybe I'll know when I get there. Or maybe I won't. I don't know. I mean, I work in a great profession. Zillions of hotels in this country. All of them need desk clerks. And I've got a good resume. No lack of job opportunities for me. I could work anywhere. So money isn't an issue. But do you think I should try? Travel, I mean. Do you think I could? I don't know. It's a big step for me. Way beyond my comfort zone. But then so is wild and crazy. Right? Thing is. We both know I'm no fan of change. Especially big changes. Really big. Like this one. Scary big. That's what it is. Insanely scary. So what do you think? Could I pull this off? Travel. Could I do it? What should I do?"

100.

My therapist smiles. "By the way," she says, "I like your hair. It's a flattering length for you. And red is definitely your color. Good choice."

101.

I wedge the last box into the backseat of my car. Books. Ouch. So heavy. Opening a smaller box, I flip through my CD collection to find the one I want. Pete Fountain. Jazz clarinet. The best of the best. Perfect music for the road. "Ready?" I say and start the car. Walter sits next to me, buckled into his car seat. I toss his toy monkey to him. He tackles it. A happy boy. On the floor is a box of fresh fruit (for me). And a big bag of treats (for Walter). Car snacks are mandatory. Ten minutes later the city of Irving fades from my rearview mirror as we head east. Southeast. Destination unknown. After a while three exit signs appear up ahead. The first will take us to

Mississippi. The second to Alabama. The third to New Orleans. "Which should we choose?" I say to Walter. "Any suggestions?" He drops his monkey and barks three times. I jerk the steering wheel. Geez! I wasn't expecting that. Such a quiet little boy. That's him. Not a barker. Not like some Chihuahuas. "Okay, then," I say. "New Orleans it is. Jazz for Christmas this year. Just like I promised." I scratch the soft fur on the top of his head. "Thanks for the advice. You're so good at that."

About the Author

Laura Stamps loves to play with words and create experimental forms for her fiction and prose poetry. She is the author of 49 novels, novellas, short story collections, and poetry books. Most recently: IT'S ALL ABOUT THE RIDE: CAT MANIA (2021, Alien Buddha Press), THE WAY OUT: 40 EMPOWERING STORIES (2022, Alien Buddha Press), and DOG DAZED: A NOVELLA (2022, Kittyfeather Press). Forthcoming: ADDICTED TO DOG MAGAZINES: A NOVELLA (Impspired, 2023). Her fiction and poetry have appeared in over 2000 magazines, anthologies, broadsides, and literary journals worldwide. She has won numerous awards, including the Muses Prize. And she is the recipient of a Pulitzer Prize nomination and 7 Pushcart Prize nominations. You can find her every day on Facebook (Laura Stamps).

Website: LauraStampsFiction.blogspot.com